MW00334660

Copyright page information:

Copyright © 2020 by The Connecting Creative, LLC

All rights reserved. No part of this book may be reproduced in any
manner whatsoever without written permission except in the case of
brief quotations embodied in critical articles and reviews.
ISBN: 978-1-7356444-0-0
First Printing, 2020

To Rose and all of the lovers of adventure

LAYLAH COPERTINO

Have you ever seen a camper?
Have you ever looked inside?

There's a kitchen and a bed and
perfect places for puppies to hide.

Have you ever seen a camper rolling down the street?

There's a driver of
that camper, a lover
of adventure,
someone quite
wonderful to meet.

Campers roll through cities and parks.
With campers you can even stop
to make s'mores in the dark!

It seems like campers can go
all over the place.

What if campers had wings we could go to different countries, we could even go to space!

If you had a camper
where would you go?
Who would come with you?
How many new people would
you get to know?

You might have a camper,
even a camper with wings,
but you don't always need a camper
to explore beautiful things.

Adventure is all around us
just waiting to begin.
The beauty of adventure is
that it happens from within.